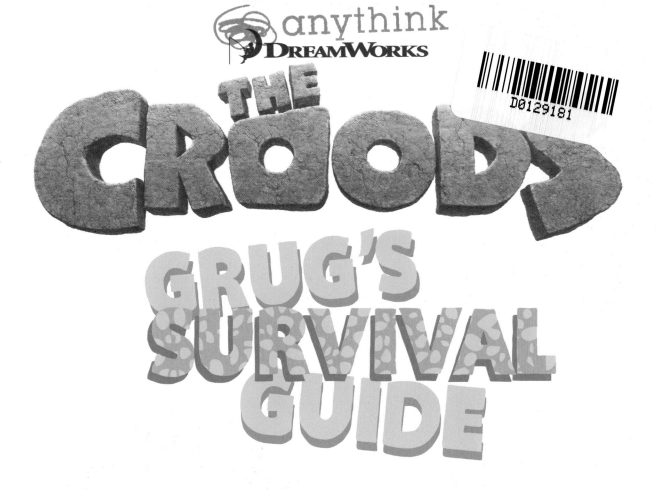

anythink

DREAMWORKS

THE CROODS
GRUG'S SURVIVAL GUIDE

adapted by Maggie Testa
based on the screenplay written by Kirk DeMicco and Chris Sanders

SIMON SPOTLIGHT
An imprint of Simon & Schuster Children's Publishing Division
New York London Toronto Sydney New Delhi
1230 Avenue of the Americas, New York, New York 10020
This Simon Spotlight edition November 2020

SIMON SPOTLIGHT and colophon are registered trademarks of Simon & Schuster, Inc. For information about special discounts for bulk purchases,
please contact Simon & Schuster Special Sales at 1-866-506-1949 or business@simonandschuster.com.
Manufactured in the United States of America 0920 LAK 2 4 6 8 10 9 7 5 3 1
ISBN 978-1-5344-8525-9 ISBN 978-1-5344-8527-3 (eBook)

CALLING ALL CAVIES

It's hard surviving in the Croodaceous period, but if Grug and the rest of the Croods can do it, so can you! Just follow the examples in this guide, and you'll be prepared for any problem this era tries to throw at you.

CAVE, SWEET CAVE

You might think it would be fun to live in a cave, but cave life isn't all it's cracked up to be. Sure, caves offer shelter, but they're also very dark and have rock-hard floors that are just plain uncomfortable to sleep on. Plus there's always the danger of catching cave fever if you're stuck in there for a few days, so you'll have to find ways to entertain yourself, just like the Croods.

GRUG TELLS THE TERRIFYING STORY OF KRISPY BEAR WHO WAS FILLED WITH CURIOSITY.

IT'S BATH NIGHT! UGGA GETS THE DUST AND BUGS OFF BY WHACKING EACH MEMBER OF HER FAMILY WITH A STICK.

EEP SOAKS UP THE LAST RAYS OF THE SETTING SUN. SHE DOESN'T LIKE THE DARK CAVE THE CROODS CALL HOME.

IT'S THE CROODS' FAMILY SLEEP PILE. SLEEP TIGHT!

GRUG'S RULES

When Grug and his family lived in their cave, they survived by following Grug's rules. It's what separated them from all the other families. You know, the families that didn't survive. These were Grug's rules:

- Anything new is bad
- Curiosity is bad
- Going out at night is bad

READY, SET, FOOD!

Every few days, your stomach will start to growl and you'll know the time has come to venture out of the cave to find food. This is easier said than done in the Croodaceous period, especially with so many fast and ferocious animals also searching for their breakfast. Always remember Grug's words of advice to his family when they went looking for food: "I want to see some real caveman action out there. We do this fast. We do this loud. We do this as a family, and never not be afraid!"

THE CROODS TRY TO SCARE OFF PREDATORS WITH THEIR THREAT DISPLAYS.

THE CROODS RUN IN BREAKFAST FORMATION AS THEY SEARCH FOR FOOD.

TODAY'S BREAKFAST IS A BIG BLUE RAMU EGG. YUM!

PERFECTING YOUR
THREAT DISPLAY

Whenever the Croods ventured out of their cave to look for food, they'd show off their threat displays to scare off any animals. They'd scowl, howl, growl, and throw their hands around wildly in the air. Grug's threat display went something like this:

"RAAAAAR! GROOOOOOOOWWWWL! ERF! ERF! GLAAAAABBBBBBLLLLLTTTTHHH!"

CRAZY CREATURES

No matter if you're living in a cave or a jungle or high up on a mountain, you must always be on the lookout for these ferocious Croodaceous creatures:

JACKROBAT: Are they bats, or are they bunnies? Who cares? Just get away from them!

LIYOTE: Very fast and very annoying, these lizard-like coyotes will try to eat your food.

BEAR OWL: Powerful and clever beasts with perfect night vision. Stay out of their way if you know what's good for you!

PIRANHAKEET: A swarm of Piranhakeets look cute, but beware. They can devour an entire Land Whale in seconds! Their weakness? They are afraid of fire.

PUNCH MONKEY: They don't look like much . . . until you see their punching paws. The secret to making them happy? Bananas, of course!

RAMU: These giant bird/beasts will stop at nothing to defend their eggs (which are delicious, if you like that sort of thing).

CUTE (BUT STILL CRAZY) CREATURES

Not every creature will be out to get you. Some of them are adorable, cuddly, and downright helpful. You might even want to turn one into a pet.

TRIP GERBIL: Sure, they get their name from their practice of trying to trip you and then stealing your food, but they're just so cute!

GIRELEPHANT: Not the friendliest creatures, but they sure are useful if you need a quick ride.

CROCOPUP: They love to play catch . . . just don't let one catch you in its jaws!

BEAR PEAR: Is that a pear, or is it a bear? These fuzzy guys are masters of the art of camouflage.

MOUSEPHANT: The size of a tiny mouse, they can roar as loudly as an elephant! Word to the wise: Wear earplugs.

MACAWNIVORE: Ginormous tigers with the coloring of macaw parrots. It's not easy, but it is possible to tame one and keep it as a pet.

FRIEND OR FOE?

If you want to know if a creature is ferocious or friendly, just ask yourself these four simple questions:

- Does it have big claws?
- Does it have big teeth?
- Is it growling at you?
- Is it about to pounce on you?

If you answered yes to any of these questions, then the only thing to do is ... **RUN!**

PLAYING WELL WITH OTHERS

Along the way, you are bound to run into other travelers at one point or another. They might have different ways of doing things. And some of those ways might even be better than your own. The trick is learning to get along.

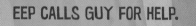

EEP CALLS GUY FOR HELP.

THIS DOES NOT MAKE
GRUG VERY HAPPY.

HOW TO TRAP A TURKEYFISH

Guy taught the Croods an easy trick that
makes finding food so much easier. All you
need is a Turkeyfish puppet and a snare.
Turkeyfish are very dumb—so dumb that
they'll follow the puppet (or you) right into
the snare. And voilà! Dinner is served!

LEARNING TO ADAPT

The most important lesson you need to learn if you're going to survive the Croodaceous period is how to adapt. Don't pay attention to the rules on the cave wall—always try new things and think of new ideas! As Grug eventually learns, never be afraid.

EEP WAVES HELLO TO SOMETHING NEW: FIRE! SHE'S NEVER SEEN IT BEFORE.

BUT IS FIRE A FRIEND . . .

. . . OR A FOE?

HEAT FROM THE FIRE TURNS GIANT CORN KERNELS INTO GIANT POPCORN. AT FIRST, GRUG DOESN'T WANT TO EAT THE GIANT POPCORN BECAUSE IT'S NEW. BUT HE SOON DISCOVERS THAT IT'S TASTY!

HOW TO GET YOURSELF ACROSS A CANYON
(WHEN ALL YOU HAVE IS FIRE, A GIANT RIB CAGE, AND SOME PIRANHAKEETS)

When Grug needed to join his family and reach safety, he came up with his first great idea. He didn't have much, but what he did have, he made use of. First he coated a giant rib cage with sticky tar. Then he lured a group of Piranhakeets to chase him into the rib cage. When he jumped into the rib cage, the Piranhakeets stuck onto it. They tried to fly free of the tar and lifted the rib cage off the ground. In order to make them fly in a straight line, Grug made use of their fear of fire to steer them. Grug was really going somewhere now!

SO THERE YOU HAVE IT:

tips and tricks for surviving the Croodaceous period. And when it all comes down to it, the most important tool for survival just might be a hug. It's another one of Grug's new ideas, and it's easy to remember. After all, it rhymes with Grug!